38 WEEKS TILL SUMMER VACATION

"A new entry in the school story sweepstakes distinguishes itself through hearty characterization and rough-and-ready kid-size humor. Fourth grade is filled with adventures for Nora Jean and her classmates: a snake in the girls' toilet, a spook house, a read-athon. . . . Kerby's overriding theme that school is fun *and* hard work is successfully integrated into the entertainingly episodic story."

—*Bulletin of the Center for Children's Books*

"A delightful book that fourth graders and others will thoroughly enjoy. Ms. Kerby has an eye for those little details that make for good storytelling." —*Children's Book Review Service*

38 Weeks Till Summer Vacation

BY MONA KERBY

Illustrated by Melodye Rosales

PUFFIN BOOKS

for Steve,
my first reader, my best friend

M.K.

PUFFIN BOOKS
Published by the Penguin Group
Penguin Books USA Inc., 375 Hudson Street, New York, New York 10014, U.S.A.
Penguin Books Ltd, 27 Wrights Lane, London W8 5TZ, England
Penguin Books Australia Ltd, Ringwood, Victoria, Australia
Penguin Books Canada Ltd, 10 Alcorn Avenue, Toronto, Ontario, Canada M4V 3B2
Penguin Books (N.Z.) Ltd, 182–190 Wairau Road, Auckland 10, New Zealand

Penguin Books Ltd, Registered Offices: Harmondsworth, Middlesex, England

First published in the United States of America by Viking Penguin,
a Division of Penguin Books USA Inc., 1989
Published in Puffin Books, 1991
3 5 7 9 10 8 6 4 2
Text copyright © Mona Kerby, 1989
Illustrations copyright © Melodye Rosales, 1989
All rights reserved

Library of Congress Catalog Card Number: 91–53105
ISBN 0-14-034205-2

Printed in the United States of America
Set in Garamond #3

Contents

1
Those Back-to-School Blues

"Welp," said Nora Jean for the fifth time that morning. "I guess this is it." She kept standing on the front porch.

"You're gonna be terrific, little lady," said Mr. Sampson.

"Gee whiz, Daddy," said Nora Jean. "Look at me. I'm not terrific. I've got freckles and flat feet."

"Go on, Nora Jean," said Mrs. Sampson. "Or you'll be late."

Nora Jean adjusted her book bag. "Welp," she said

for the sixth time. "See you around." Then she turned and walked down the street toward school.

At the corner, Rosalie Chester was waiting for Nora Jean. Nora Jean waved. No matter what, Rosalie never got mad at Nora Jean. Anything that Nora Jean did or said was perfectly fine with her.

Their friendship began in third grade on the first day of school. When Nora Jean accidentally dropped her pencil, Rosalie reached across the aisle to pick it up. Jimmy Lee Drover grinned and sang, "I see Fatty-Pants' underwear." Rosalie's face turned beet-red, but she pretended not to hear. Right then and there, Nora Jean decided to be friends with Rosalie.

Rosalie was as fat as Nora Jean was skinny. It was a perfect friendship. Still, Rosalie was Nora Jean's second best friend.

"Hey there," said Rosalie.

"Hey yourself," said Nora Jean. "Listen to this. I've just made up a new song."

"Boo-hoo, I've got those back-to-school blues.

You, too, you've got those back-to-school blues."

"That's swell, Nora Jean," said Rosalie.

"I thought you'd like it," said Nora Jean.

The two friends sang their song all the way to school. On Briley Street, Chip Smith fell in behind them and started singing along, too.

A crowd had already gathered at the school bike

rack. Thomasina Reeves had a new bike and she was showing it off.

Nora Jean thought that Thomasina was the most beautiful person in the whole world. For one thing, Thomasina wasn't skinny. Besides that, she had amazing eyes. One eye was deep-sea blue and the other was grass green. Somehow, they made Nora Jean's brown eyes seem plain.

Thomasina had curly red hair and a turned-up nose. When she sweated, she had these wonderful little sweat droplets on the end of her nose. More than anything, Nora Jean wanted to sweat like Thomasina Reeves.

Nora Jean wished that her straight brown hair looked exactly like Thomasina's. In fact, Nora Jean wished that she was Thomasina. Thomasina was Nora Jean's very best friend.

"Hi, Thomasina," said Nora Jean.

Thomasina looked at Nora Jean's feet. "I see your mother bought you some new corrective shoes," said Thomasina.

"Uh, yeah," said Nora Jean, trying to hide her feet behind a bicycle tire.

"Hey, everybody," said Chip. "Wait till you hear the song Nora Jean made up."

Chip began snapping his fingers and swaying to the beat. Soon, everybody at the bike rack began wailing the *Back-to-School Blues*. That was when Jimmy Lee arrived.

Jimmy Lee Drover was the biggest kid at R. B. Nolen Elementary. He was taller than the librarian. The gym teacher looked like a shrimp next to the giant fourth grader. Jimmy Lee didn't talk much, but he did like to tease. Nobody liked to mess with Jimmy Lee. After all, he was big.

"Hey, Fatty-Pants, you jiggle when you wiggle," said Jimmy Lee.

Rosalie pretended not to hear, but her eyes grew wide and she kept them on Nora Jean.

Jimmy Lee moved in between the two friends. He faced Rosalie. "Boogy some more," he said.

The kids grew silent. One or two of them started walking toward the door. Thomasina pulled on Nora Jean's arm. "Come on, Nora Jean," she said. "Let's go inside."

Nora Jean's heart was beating fast. She loved it when Thomasina noticed her. Why should she worry about Rosalie? After all, Rosalie was just her second best friend. Why not go on inside with Thomasina, she thought.

Nora Jean took a deep breath and stepped toward Jimmy Lee. She looked up.

"Buzz off," she said.

"Says who?" he said. Jimmy Lee grinned. Nora Jean could see all his teeth, even his fillings.

"Says the kid with the kicking corrective shoes," said Nora Jean. She began to tap dance. Nora Jean shuffled, hopped, and kicked. She waved her arms. She shook her head. She danced all around Jimmy Lee. At the top of her lungs she sang, "I've got those back-to-school blues!"

The bell rang. Nora Jean never knew if it was her courage, her shoes, or the bell that saved them, but Jimmy Lee let them go.

Nora Jean spent the next moments in a daze. She heard laughter. She felt pats on her back. And she thought she heard Chip Smith say, "Way to go, Sampson shoes!"

Somehow she made it into the right fourth grade classroom and found a seat.

Gradually, Nora Jean focused her attention on the teacher. Her name was Mrs. Carter. She was about medium height. She wasn't skinny, but she wasn't fat either.

Her stomach pooched out and she wore teacher shoes. She had short dark brown hair with bangs. She had something white in her hair. Nora Jean couldn't tell if it was gray hair or chalk.

Nora Jean had almost decided that Mrs. Carter was

just another ordinary teacher. But then she looked into her eyes. They were amazing. Mrs. Carter's big brown eyes could change from twinkly happy to angry black to wide-open surprise. Why, I didn't know that eyes could talk, she thought. By staring at her teacher's face, Nora Jean found herself listening to every word that she said.

Mrs. Carter cleared her throat. "I want to welcome you all to the fourth grade at R. B. Nolen Elementary School of Fort Worth, Texas." This year, you will work hard. You will read more, study more, write more, and learn more than you ever have in your entire life. It won't be easy. But I promise you one thing. At the end of this year, you will love school.

"Now. Sit up straight. When I call your name, raise your hand and say, 'Here.' "

This just isn't my day, Nora Jean thought to herself. During roll call, she looked at the other kids. At least Thomasina and Rosalie were in her room. Chip Smith grinned at her. Rex Thompson was in the row by the windows. She saw some other kids she knew.

When it came time for Will Klein to answer, he didn't say, "Here." Instead, as he raised his hand, he said, "There's only thirty-eight more weeks till summer vacation."

Mrs. Carter stopped and looked surprised. Then,

she laughed out loud. "If you don't count the two weeks of winter holidays, you are correct, Mr. Klein," she replied.

After calling the roll, Mrs. Carter said, "We're missing only one person."

The door opened. Jimmy Lee Drover walked in. "Ah, you must be Jimmy Lee," said Mrs. Carter. She smiled. "We've been expecting you." As she bent down to mark him present, Jimmy Lee caught Nora Jean's eye. He mouthed the words, "I'm gonna get you."

Nora Jean gulped. Thirty-eight weeks till summer vacation was going to be a very long time.

2
Live from the
Girls Bathroom

Mrs. Carter was right. Fourth grade was hard. Nora
Jean wrote so much with her pencil that she had a
permanent pink bump on her third finger.

But it wasn't the usual boring ditto papers. Instead,
they did group projects, independent projects, plays,
and library research. They worked on the computers,
and they were always doing science experiments. Last
year, Mrs. Chutney just read the science book aloud.
When she came to an experiment, Mrs. Chutney told
the class to shut their eyes and pretend they were

doing them. Afterward, she would say, "Now, wasn't that fun, boys and girls?"

Mrs. Carter was different. For one thing, she read real books to them. Watching Mrs. Carter's face and listening to her voice was almost as good as television. Everybody laughed when Mrs. Carter read the *Soup* books and the *Hank the Cowdog* stories. Everybody cried when Mrs. Carter read *Where the Red Fern Grows.* Even Jimmy Lee.

Mrs. Carter looked strict, but she didn't yell at them like other teachers did. Nora Jean was sort of scared of her teacher, and it seemed to Nora Jean that the other kids were, too. It was funny how you could be scared of a teacher you liked, thought Nora Jean.

Some days, Nora Jean almost liked school. But one look at her finger bump or Jimmy Lee and she would change her mind.

One hot afternoon in September, right before recess, Mrs. Carter said, "I need someone to clean the erasers. Do I have a volunteer?"

Practically everybody raised a hand. Nora Jean stretched her hand high and wriggled her fingers just a little. She knew that Mrs. Carter didn't like floppy arm wavers.

"All right, Nora Jean," said Mrs. Carter. "You may go."

Nora Jean smiled. The slight finger wiggle had done the trick. She turned to smile at Thomasina, but she looked mad.

"Uh, Mrs. Carter," said Nora Jean. "Can I have a helper?"

"Why, I suppose so," said Mrs. Carter.

Nora Jean started to say she wanted Thomasina, but she never got the chance.

"Chip, you may help, also," said Mrs. Carter.

Chip followed Nora Jean outside. Together, they beat the erasers on the side of the building. They beat them on the sidewalk. Then they slapped the erasers like tambourines. September afternoons were perfect for beating erasers.

"Beating erasers is my favorite thing to do," said Chip. "I wonder if Mrs. Carter knows that." He had chalk on his jeans, his shirt, and his face.

"Mine, too," said Nora Jean. "Except for lunch."

"Oh, yeah, I forgot about that," said Chip.

From where they stood, they could see the first graders playing.

"See that kid with the baseball cap?" said Chip. "That's Jimmy Lee's little brother."

"I didn't know he had a brother," said Nora Jean.

"Uh-huh. I got a little brother in first grade. Benny said that one day after school, Jimmy Lee told the first grade boys that any kid who touched his brother was chopped liver."

"I wonder why Jimmy Lee is so mean," said Nora Jean. She was throwing erasers up and catching them.

"Rex Thompson gave me three dollars last year if I would beat up Jimmy Lee for him," said Chip.

"Wow," said Nora. Rex Thompson was the shortest and pudgiest kid in the class. He talked with a low raspy voice. Nora Jean thought Rex looked like an overgrown teddy bear. She never talked to him much, but she liked him all right.

"Did you keep the money?" asked Nora Jean.

"No, I talked it over with my uncle. He goes to Richland High and he picks me and Benny up after school every day."

"Well, what did your uncle say?" asked Nora Jean.

"He said that I shouldn't judge Jimmy Lee until I walked a mile in his moccasins or something like that."

"What's that supposed to mean?" asked Nora Jean.

"Beats me," answered Chip. "Since he started high school, he's always saying weird stuff like that."

Nora Jean and Chip stood around some more. After a while, Nora Jean figured it was time to go in.

Inside, Nora Jean stopped by the bathroom while Chip played with the water fountain. Nora Jean took one look at the toilet and started screaming. "Chip, come here!" she yelled. She flushed the toilet. Nothing happened.

Chip stood beside the bathroom door. "Gee whiz, Nora Jean. I can't go in the girls' bathroom."

"You're gonna miss it if you don't!" she yelled.

Nora Jean flushed the toilet again. It didn't disappear. "Wow," she muttered. She was scared and excited at the same time. Nothing like this had ever happened at R. B. Nolen before.

"Chip!" Nora Jean yelled. "This may be your last chance!"

Nora Jean heard Chip tiptoe into the girls' bathroom. Together they stood and stared at the toilet bowl.

A big black snake stared back at them.

That's when the commotion started. The girls walked in for their afternoon bathroom break. Some of them started screaming when they saw a boy in the girls' bathroom. Other girls started screaming when they saw the snake. Mrs. Carter marched into the bathroom to restore order. But when she saw the snake, she screamed, too.

Somebody fetched Mr. Brown, the custodian. Then somebody ran for Mr. Miller, the principal. Mr. Brown and Mr. Miller took turns flushing. The snake wouldn't flush. With every flush, it raised its head almost a foot out of the toilet bowl.

Nora Jean heard sirens. Soon, big, husky firemen walked into the girls' bathroom of R. B. Nolen. And right behind them stood a Channel 5 reporter and cameraman. Nora Jean counted. There were seventeen girls, one boy, and eight grown-ups in the bathroom.

Nora Jean grinned. "This is terrific," she said.

By that time, Mrs. Carter had regained her composure.

"Girls, uh, Chip, you too. Let's leave these gentlemen. Follow me," she said.

Nora Jean did not want to follow her teacher, and from the looks on the other kids' faces, they felt the same way. Teachers sure know how to ruin a good time, Nora Jean thought to herself.

Back in class, Mrs. Carter told the boys and girls to get out their library books. Nora Jean had barely opened her book when Mr. Miller walked in and whispered something to Mrs. Carter.

"Nora Jean. Chip. Please go with Mr. Miller," she said.

Nora Jean's heart pounded. Were they in trouble?

In the hall, Chip said, "Mr. Miller, Nora Jean and I didn't put the snake in the toilet, honest. And I'm sorry for going in the girls' bathroom, but I thought Nora Jean was gonna puke. Honest."

"What's that?" said Mr. Miller, straightening his tie. He seemed to be thinking about something else. "Oh, sure I understand. Listen, kids. That Channel 5 reporter wants to ask you a few questions on camera. You'll be representing the Nolen 'Gators, so be on your best behavior, okay?"

Nora Jean looked at Mr. Miller. She gulped. "Yes, sir."

The reporter wanted to film the story in the bathroom. So Mr. Miller, Chip, and Nora Jean lined up in front of the stalls. Behind them, the firemen were working on the toilet.

"Roll 'em, Rich," said the reporter. "Good afternoon, folks. We're standing here in the girls' bathroom of R. B. Nolen Elementary School. A most unusual event occurred here today. It seems that a rattlesnake from the sewer swam up the pipes into one of the toilets.

"Yes, folks, it's true. On my left is a would-be victim of the snake. Well, little girl, what do you have to say?"

Nora Jean cleared her throat. "It was a sight to behold."

"And, little boy, I take it you rushed in to aid a

damsel in distress. What do you have to say for yourself?" asked the reporter.

"I wish we could have snakes in the toilet every day," said Chip.

"Ho-ho, out of the mouths of babes. Also standing with us today is the principal of R. B. Nolen Elementary, Mr. Eugene Miller," said the reporter. "Speak your words of wisdom, Mr. Principal."

Mr. Miller fiddled with his tie and pulled up his pants. "Uh, yes, Chris. We try to provide all kinds of learning experiences here at R. B. Nolen Elementary."

"Well, well," said the reporter. "And who said Texas couldn't improve its schools."

"Got it!" shouted one of the firemen.

"Come closer, folks. I believe we're about to make headway into the snake escapade," said the reporter. Then he stepped in the bathroom stall with the three firemen. Nora Jean had never seen four grown men inside one bathroom stall.

"And now, brave firemen, tell the viewers at home about your progress with the deadly sewer snake," said the reporter.

"Well, sir," said the tallest one. He spit some tobacco juice in the toilet, then removed his fire helmet and wiped the sweat from his forehead. "We tried flushing, but that didn't work. Then Bill here tried stompin' it to death with his boot, but that didn't work neither. A shovel finally did the trick for us. We've just now sliced its head off."

"Eew, gross," said Chip.

"Hush, kid," whispered the reporter. "And so, once again, our firemen have saved us." He saluted the fireman who was holding the shovel. "This is Chris Carson, Action 5 News. Back to you, Brad."

"Wrap it up, Rich," said the reporter to the cameraman. "Well, folks, that's show biz. Don't miss the six o'clock news. Catch you later."

Then Chris Carson, Action 5 reporter, left the girls' bathroom of the R. B. Nolen Elementary School.

3

Snakes and Spaghetti

At six o'clock that evening, every television set on Cylinda Sue Circle was tuned in to see Nora Jean. Later, the phone rang for most of the night. The neighbors called. Aunt Mary Lynn called. Grandmother and Granddaddy Robertson called. Grandmother and Granddaddy Rudd called. They were all proud of their little girl.

Mr. Sampson videotaped the snake story segment so that they could watch their darling Nora Jean over and over again. Mrs. Sampson served popcorn. After the twelfth time, Mr. Sampson stood up and belched. "That's my little tiger!" he said.

Nora Jean's heart soared. On the way to the bathtub, Nora Jean turned ballerina circles. Never had her hall shadow looked so graceful. Her long skinny arms waved in the air. Her long skinny legs leaped off the ground. She only tripped a couple of times. After all, toe points were very difficult to do in corrective shoes.

In bed, as she drifted off to sleep, Nora Jean decided that since she was now a famous person, she really must practice her autograph.

For the next few weeks, the fourth graders talked about the snake in the toilet. They felt special because it happened in their grade. Usually, the sixth graders got to do all the neat stuff.

Nora Jean could hardly wait to get to school in the mornings. They studied snakes in class. They read snake books. They wrote snake stories. They examined snake skins and rattles. They even did snake math problems. As Mrs. Carter said, "It's not every day that a snake swims up the sewer to school."

One Wednesday in the middle of October, the subject of snakes was once again the topic of conversation at the lunch table.

Wednesdays were spaghetti days at R. B. Nolen Elementary. Some kids in Mrs. Carter's class brought their lunches. But most of them slumped in front of their trays, slurping up their spaghetti.

"You know," said Will Klein as he sucked up a long piece, "spaghetti looks like snakes."

"Don't you have any manners?" asked Thomasina. In a prim and proper way, she wrapped her spaghetti around her plastic spoon.

Nora Jean tried to have good manners like Thomasina, but every time she wrapped her spaghetti around her spoon, it fell off. After a couple of times, she gave up. Too many manners could starve a person to death.

"Hey," said Chip. "Tell us about the snake again, Nora Jean."

Nora Jean sat up a little straighter and finished slurping a piece of spaghetti. "Well, it all began when the snake reared its ugly head and hissed at me."

"How did it hiss?" asked Rosalie.

"Like this," said Chip, making a hissing sound. "And it rattled, too."

"I saw y'all on television," said Rex Thompson. He was eating a frozen peanut butter sandwich.

Kids who forgot their lunch money were given a frozen sandwich. Students at R. B. Nolen never go hungry, Mr. Miller always said. They just break their teeth, Nora Jean thought.

"You sure did look good on television, Nora Jean,"

said Chip. "You oughta think about a TV career."

Nora Jean was flattered. "Oh, you really think so?" she said. She smoothed down her bangs with the hand that didn't have spaghetti sauce on it.

Jimmy Lee grinned.

"You looked like a jerk," he said.

The lunch table grew quiet. The only sounds were the plastic forks and spoons scraping the cardboard trays.

"Yeah," said Jimmy Lee Drover in a louder voice. "You and Chip and old man Miller looked like the Three Stooges." By now, Jimmy Lee was laughing so hard that tears came to his eyes.

"Leave Nora Jean alone," said Chip.

"What's the matter? You gotta crush on Toothpick Legs, Smith?" asked Lee, wiping his cheeks.

Chip's face turned bright red. He lunged across the table and smashed his roll in Jimmy Lee's face. Jimmy Lee grabbed Chip's arms.

"Drover and Smith!" shouted Mrs. Pinker, the lunchroom monitor. "Throw your trays away and head for the troublemakers' table. And I mean *move it!*"

Both of the lunchroom monitors were nice ladies outside the cafeteria. But during lunch, they acted as if they were in charge of a war zone.

After a few minutes, Rex Thompson said in a low voice, "Boy, do I hate Jimmy Lee."

Rex continued. "The snake should have been in the boys' bathroom and Jimmy Lee should have pulled his britches down and sat on it. Boy, I sure do wish the snake had bitten Jimmy Lee on the behind."

The kids began to laugh and poke each other and soon the lunchroom sounds were back to the normal roar.

Nora Jean, however, was quiet. One thought kept racing through her mind. Toothpick legs. Jimmy Lee has just told the whole world that I've got toothpick legs.

4
The Spook House

The week before Halloween, Mrs. Carter made a wonderful announcement. Our class, she said with a smile, will be in charge of the Spook House.

Excitement danced inside Nora Jean. She began to fidget. She looked around the room. Everyone was grinning and wiggling. Chip, with his hands clasped above his head, was acting like a winning athlete.

The entire class was happy, except for one person. In the back seat of the last row, Nora Jean saw Jimmy Lee scowling. His hand shot up in the air.

"What about the little kids?" asked Jimmy Lee.

"Pardon me?" asked Mrs. Carter. Her face and eyes seemed puzzled.

Whenever Jimmy Lee said something in class, Mrs. Carter listened with interest and treated him with respect. Of course, that's how she treated the other students. But why, Nora Jean wondered, was Mrs. Carter nice to Jimmy Lee? Didn't her teacher realize that he was mean? Nora Jean snorted. Toothpick legs—the very idea.

"I don't want to be a part of no Spook House," Jimmy Lee said gruffly. " 'Cause I don't want to be scaring no little kids."

"Hmm," said Mrs. Carter. "Interesting point." She stood still and gazed out the windows.

"How about this," asked Mrs. Carter, after several minutes. "Why don't you be the Spook House guard? Your job will be to keep things running smoothly and to keep an eye on the little ones. Think it over."

The kids in Mrs. Carter's class gave up recess to work on the Spook House. As Mrs. Carter had explained, "I can fit snakes into the curriculum, but there's no place in the state guidelines for spook houses."

At 5:30 Saturday evening, Nora Jean was ready for the carnival. She took one last look in the bathroom mirror. She was pleased. Yep, she thought to herself.

Three hours in a locked bathroom can work miracles.

Her brown hair was now vivid pink. It stuck straight up. Her eyelids were covered with glitter and purple eye shadow. On her cheeks, she had drawn jagged bolts of silver lightning. Her lips were green. Each fake fingernail was ruby red and two inches long. She wore her black ballet leotard and tights. Nora Jean was truly transformed. Only one thing gave her away. On her feet, she wore her corrective shoes.

When Nora Jean walked into the kitchen, her mother screamed. "Go clean yourself up right now!"

Nora Jean wailed, but she didn't cry. She wasn't about to mess up her makeup.

"What's all this commotion?" asked Mr. Sampson. He came in from the backyard where he had been raking the leaves.

Mr. Sampson made his wife sit down at the kitchen table. He rubbed her back. "Times have changed, Viola," he said. "Times have changed." Mr. Sampson motioned for his daughter to go. Nora Jean was off in a flash.

Jimmy Lee was already standing guard at the classroom door. He was not wearing a costume. Instead, he wore his everyday jeans, cowboy shirt, and dirty tennis shoes. Spoilsport, Nora Jean thought to herself.

Nora Jean did her best to walk past him with the

air of an exotic beauty. She tripped on the door ledge.

Jimmy Lee sneered. "You look like a burnt pencil, Sampson," he said.

But Nora Jean only held her head higher and sniffed. Tonight was Halloween and Nora Jean the vamp tramp was not about to let Jimmy Lee spoil the evening.

The rest of the kids were already in their places. Rex, with his dracula fangs and cape, was practicing his wicked "Good evening" and his scary laugh. Will Klein was stretched out on the table pretending to be a dead mummy.

Rosalie was a ghost. She was in charge of the "Feel and Smell the Dead Mummy" table. She had four boxes with holes cut out of the top. The first box held mummy blood (mayonnaise). The second box held mummy eyeballs (peeled grapes). The third held worms that ate the mummy (spaghetti). The last box held the smell of the dead mummy (smashed cockroaches).

Chip Smith stood at the empty refrigerator box. The box was painted black and had the ends cut out. Chip was dressed as Frankenstein. He was supposed to scare the kids as they crawled into the tunnel and scare them again when they crawled out.

Nora Jean gasped when she saw Thomasina. She

wore a short tight skirt. Two beach balls were stuck inside her blouse. She looked like Dolly Parton. Nora Jean sighed. She wished that she, too, could look like Dolly Parton.

"Class," said Mrs. Carter. "Best of luck tonight. Remember, I'll be down the hall at the ticket booth if you need me. Positions, everyone!"

Nora Jean and Thomasina made their way to the door. They were the Spook House guides for the evening. Nora Jean would lead, and Thomasina would be at the rear of the group.

"Don't worry," said Thomasina, adjusting her blouse, "If someone causes trouble, I'll just bump 'em with my beach balls."

When Nora Jean opened the door, she saw a line of students already waiting to enter the Spook House. She let the first group in and Thomasina took their tickets. The little kids stared at Nora Jean's pink punk hairdo and at Thomasina's beach balls. None of them said a word. Nora Jean smiled wickedly. The Spook House was open for business.

With her most evil voice, Nora Jean spoke. "Step right in, ghosts and goblins."

Thomasina slammed the door with a loud bang. The little kids jumped.

"For the scariest adventure twenty-five cents can

buy," Nora Jean continued, "bid your friends and neighbors adiós, because you probably won't get out of here alive. Never before have humans witnessed such dreadful, frightful, terrifying events. Follow me close, my lovelies, because only my pets survive." Then Nora Jean widened her green lips and screamed. "Aaa-eee---iii--ooo-uuuuuuu!"

The little kids lunged for Nora Jean. Hands pulled at her tights. Together, like quivering jellyfish, they walked through the Spook House. When Nora Jean told them to touch, the little kids touched. When she told them to smell, they smelled. Some whimpered. Some shivered. One or two giggled. But all of them obeyed Nora Jean.

After they had crawled through Frankenstein's tunnel and escaped Chip's pinching knee hold, Nora Jean threw back her head and howled.

"You live, my lovelies," she wailed. "Get out quick before I eat you! Aaa-eee---iii--ooo-uuuuuu!"

All night, Nora Jean repeated her performance. With each new group, the vamp tramp improved her evil voice and her beady-eyed stare.

She was a little worried about her makeup. She had wiped the sweat from her face so much that her hands were now covered with purple, green, and silver paint. Nora Jean kept picking glitter off her tongue. But her dripping colors did not seem to affect the Spook House business. Every time she opened the door, the line was longer.

So, when Nora Jean greeted another group of first graders, she had no reason to suspect that anything would go wrong. Jimmy Lee growled at her and told her to cool it, but he had been telling her that all night.

Right from the start, one kid gave her problems. He cried when he saw Dracula. He cried when he saw the ghost. He refused to touch anything at the "Feel the Dead Mummy" table. But the real ruckus started at Frankenstein's tunnel. Nora Jean told him to crawl. Instead, he lay down on the floor, kicked his feet, and screamed bloody murder.

"I want Jimmy Lee!" he yelled.

Jimmy Lee was there in a second and he was furious. "What do you mean scaring my little brother, Sampson?"

How dare Jimmy Lee be mean to her, thought Nora Jean. She was only doing her job.

She stamped her foot and shouted. "First of all, I didn't know he was your little brother. If I had, I wouldn't have let him in. Secondly, in case you haven't noticed, this is a Spook House. When you walk in this door, you're gonna get a quarter's worth of scare.

It's not my fault you and your little brother don't appreciate my talents."

Nora Jean took a deep breath and continued. "For your information, Jimmy Lee Drover, I'm the best vamp tramp you'll ever see!"

Jimmy Lee scowled at Nora Jean. "Tramp is right," he muttered. "Tell Mrs. Carter I quit. Me and Frankie are going home."

Jimmy Lee gently picked up his brother and wiped away his tears. Then, with his arms wrapped tightly around his brother, Jimmy Lee walked out the Spook House door.

5
26 Weeks to Go

Winter came to Texas. Although it wasn't really cold in Fort Worth, Mr. and Mrs. Sampson said that it was the rainiest, cloudiest November that they remembered.

The long days at school seemed to match the drizzling rain. Snake math had been fun. But no matter how exciting some things were at school, there was always going to be seat work, board work, homework, and tests.

Of course, Nora Jean knew one reason why school was so boring. After the Halloween Spook House,

Nora Jean made a promise to herself. For the rest of her life, she was not going to look at or speak to Jimmy Lee Drover.

She tried not to break her promise more than once a day.

Nora Jean broke it every single time Jimmy Lee called her Toothpick Legs. She had to. Nora Jean puffed up like a frog, crossed her arms over her stomach, and gave Jimmy Lee a cold, black, beady-eyed stare.

This was one of the first looks Mrs. Carter had taught the class. She said it was body language and it meant, "Correct your behavior on the double." The look scared Nora Jean. Since it worked for Mrs. Carter, Nora Jean used it on Jimmy Lee. Jimmy Lee always laughed. Still, Nora Jean knew that deep inside, Jimmy Lee was shaking in his tennis shoes.

She also broke her promise not to stare at Jimmy Lee when he told Mrs. Carter it would be a cold day in h--- before he'd wear a turkey suit.

One afternoon, Mrs. Carter announced that the fourth grade was in charge of the November PTA program.

"Let's see," said Mrs. Carter. "Thomasina will play the piano. Nora Jean will recite the poem. And the class will sing. All we need now is the turkey."

34

"Jimmy Lee is a turkey," someone muttered from the back of the room. Nora Jean wasn't sure, but it sounded like Rex.

Jimmy Lee turned red in the face. He jumped out of his chair and roared. "Who was the slime bucket that said that?"

The whole class stared in openmouthed surprise. The slime bucket didn't say a word.

Nora Jean never knew if Jimmy Lee actually said any curse words or not. In the commotion, she couldn't hear. Jimmy Lee was hollering and getting redder in the face by the minute. Mrs. Carter dropped her note pad, and jumped over two chairs to get to him. She started rubbing his back and saying, "There, there." All the theres drowned out any possible curse words. Nora Jean was a little disappointed.

Eventually Mrs. Carter restored order. Rex Thompson agreed to be the turkey.

On the first Monday in December, Will Klein announced that there were twenty-six more weeks until summer vacation. Including all holidays, he added. To Nora Jean, twenty-six weeks might just as well have been twenty-six years. I'll be a toothless old woman before I ever get out of fourth grade, she thought.

There was one thing, however, that helped pass the time in school—making soap dogs.

In December, students at R. B. Nolen Elementary made presents for their parents. Even though all the parents had to go to the store, select the necessary materials, pay for them, and send them to school in a sack, Nora Jean's parents always acted surprised on Christmas day. "How did you know that this was just what we were wanting?" they would ask. In these moments, Nora Jean's parents seemed so happy, she never had the heart to explain the cold hard facts to them.

One year Nora Jean had given her parents a plaster of Paris imprint of her hand. It cracked and Nora Jean cried. But Mr. and Mrs. Sampson told their daughter that they had been wanting a cracked plaster of Paris hand for a long time. Another year, Nora Jean made a doorknob decoration out of green felt. Mr. Sampson said, "Doorknob decorations can sure get a fella in the Christmas spirit."

Every afternoon, as Nora Jean worked on her soap dog, she could almost hear her father say, "Why, lookie here, Viola. We got us a soap dog." Nora Jean chewed on her tongue and worked harder.

While Nora Jean huddled over her desk, she practiced a little speech inside her head. She knew that her parents would want to hear how their very wonderful daughter had made this very, very wonderful gift for them.

Nora Jean talked to people a lot inside her head. In fact, it was the best way to talk to people because they always listened.

"Not just anybody can make a good soap dog," she said in her silent speech. "The first thing you need is a bar of soap. This has to be new soap and it has to be a large bar, or else your dog will look like a mutt. And it can't be the bargain brand that Mama buys. This bar has to be the expensive kind, the stuff with cold cream.

"The next thing you need is a washcloth. That's a fancy way of saying washrag. You gotta have a new one, and it can't be too thick or too thin. You also gotta color coordinate your rag and soap bar. Whoever heard of a yellow-bodied dog with green legs? The best soap dogs are pink.

"Now comes the hard part. Take the washcloth. Roll one long side toward the middle. Do the same to the other side. If you do it right, you have two long cigarlike rolls. Place the rolls right side up on the soap. The rolls go the same direction as the long part of the soap.

"The rolls become the two front legs, the dog's top side, and the hind legs. Stick one pin through each roll into the ends of the soap. This means you gotta use four pins.

"On one end of the soap, attach sequined eyes on

the cigar rolls. Cut felt ears, felt tongue, and felt tail. Glue them on just so and Ta-da! You have a beautiful soap dog made by your loving daughter's hands!"

Every day, as Nora Jean practiced her speech, she could almost feel her parents' hugs and kisses. Without a doubt, this was the most wonderful present she had ever made.

Two days before the holidays, the soap dogs sat on the window ledge and stared at the class with their sequined eyes. Nora Jean liked to look at hers. It was the best one.

The worst looking soap dog belonged to Jimmy Lee. His washcloth was stiff and dirty white. His bar of soap was the kind they used at school.

Mrs. Carter had offered him a prettier washcloth and a larger bar of soap. Jimmy Lee shook his head no. Jimmy Lee sure was stubborn sometimes. At lunch, whenever he forgot his money, he never took a free sandwich. Instead, he didn't eat. He sat with his arms crossed, and glared at anybody who looked his way.

After the party was over, on the last day of school, the excitement still crackled in Mrs. Carter's classroom. Nora Jean crammed the third cupcake in her mouth. She felt great.

She popped open her grocery sack and scooted the

party treats inside. She could leave as soon as she finished.

"Nora Jean," said Thomasina, in her most sugary sweet voice.

Nora Jean looked up. Her head was stuck between her legs. She was checking her desk one more time. "Yeah," she said.

"Carry my soap dog to my bike while I carry my sack," she said. "I don't want it to get messed up." Thomasina shook her red curls. "You can come back later and get your stuff."

For a minute, Nora Jean was irritated with her best friend. After all, she thought to herself, Thomasina had two hands. But if Nora Jean said no, Thomasina might not like her anymore. Nora Jean sighed. "Okay, but let's hurry."

Nora Jean left the bike rack in a flash. As she raced down the hall, she saw Jimmy Lee leaving the classroom. He waved and grinned at her.

The empty room was dark and quiet. The sound of Nora Jean's heavy breathing filled the room. When she reached the window ledge, her heart seemed to stop.

Jimmy Lee's soap dog was the only one left. And then, Nora Jean knew. Jimmy Lee had stolen her present. Quickly she stuffed her sack in her book bag and ran out the door. She almost knocked down Mrs. Carter.

"Oh, I'm glad I saw you, Nora Jean," said Mrs. Carter. "Jimmy Lee asked me to give you a message. He said to tell you thanks and Merry Christmas." Mrs. Carter smoothed Nora Jean's hair. "Knowing you, you probably did something very nice. Merry Christmas, dear."

Nora Jean walked home alone. She stuffed her hands in her pockets and walked stoop-shouldered to balance her lumpy book bag on her back. She clinched her teeth and sang a song. "Jingle bells, shotgun shells, soap dog's gone away."

This was it. Nora Jean had had enough. For the rest of her life, she was never, ever going to forgive Jimmy Lee.

6

Nancy Drew Dreams

On Christmas morning, Mr. Sampson opened his present from Nora Jean. "Why lookie here, Viola. We got us some potholders." He beamed at his little girl. "How did you know that's just what we've been wanting?"

Mrs. Sampson smiled, too. "Oh, Elbert, aren't they beautiful? Such pretty colors and designs. And look, Nora Jean even finished off the edges."

"Well, I'll be," said Mr. Sampson. Mrs. Sampson hugged their daughter. Mr. Sampson patted her on the back.

Nora Jean sighed. Potholders were not as elegant as soap dogs, but it was the best she could do on short notice.

During the winter holidays, there were new toys to play with, family to visit, and good food to eat. She didn't see her friends much. Thomasina was visiting her grandmother in Oklahoma, and Rosalie's cousins were up from San Antonio.

But even though this was the season of peace, Nora Jean did not forgive Jimmy Lee. Every night after she said her prayers, she made a wish. "I hope Jimmy Lee's soap dog falls in the toilet and drowns."

"Nora Jean," Mrs. Sampson said one morning as she sat at the kitchen table and read the newspaper. "Hurry up and get dressed. The stores are advertising sales. Let's go buy you a new winter coat."

"Okay!" said Nora Jean, heading to her room. "I'll be ready in a jumping jack flash!"

Nora Jean's coat was two years old. She had outgrown it. But the size didn't bother her. She wanted a new one because her old one looked like a baby coat.

The Sampsons were on a budget because they were saving for Nora Jean's college education. One way Mrs. Sampson saved money was by shopping at sales. This meant that Nora Jean usually got short sets in

September and coats when winter was nearly over. Her mother bought everything too large. It was up to Nora Jean to grow into her clothes at the right time.

Whenever Mrs. Sampson found a really good sale, she would get all excited and say, "With the money we saved, we bought you a college textbook and three pencils."

Most of the time Nora Jean would get excited, too. But every so often, she wished that she could have her clothes at the right season instead of saving for so many college pencils.

When Nora Jean and her mother arrived at the shopping mall, they started at one end and worked their way to the other end. Nora Jean tried on the coats that she liked as well as the ones that her mother liked. Then Nora Jean stood in front of the three-way mirror and turned circles.

First, Mrs. Sampson checked to see if there was plenty of material in the hem so that she could let it out when Nora Jean grew taller. Then she looked to see if the coat was suitable for school and for church. Last but not least, Mrs. Sampson checked to see if the price was right.

Nora Jean really didn't care about any of these things. She just wanted a coat with pizzazz. She wanted a coat that made her look grown-up and so-phisticated. After all, she was practically a preteen.

Finally, in the seventh store, Nora Jean found the perfect coat. It was bright red, her favorite color. Instead of buttoning, it wrapped around with a belt that tied in the front.

Nora Jean pushed up the collar and tightened the belt. She looked at herself in the mirror. She felt a tingle of excitement. I look exactly like Nancy Drew, she thought.

This year, Nora Jean had started reading Nancy Drew books. At school, Mrs. Carter had a shelf of Nancy Drew books which she had read when she was a little girl. Whenever Nora Jean finished her work, she read one of her teacher's old mysteries. Nancy Drew led a far more exciting life than Nora Jean.

But this was a detective coat. Nora Jean imagined herself solving mysteries. With this coat, she too could live an exciting life. She would be famous. Someday little girls would be reading Nora Jean Sampson mystery books.

"Mama, this is the coat I want," said Nora Jean.

"Come here and let's see." Mrs. Sampson checked the hem.

"Look, it has lots of material at the hem," said Nora Jean. "You can let it out a bunch of times. Since it doesn't button, I can get real fat. Why, I can probably wear this coat when I go to college."

"Is that right?" Mrs. Sampson said. "Well, you do look pretty in it. Red is certainly your color. How much is it?"

Nora Jean held up her arm with the price tag. Please let the price be right, she wished.

"Why, Nora Jean. This coat isn't on sale," said Mrs. Sampson. "Someone must have accidentally placed a regular priced coat on the sales rack."

Mrs. Sampson straightened up. "Let's keep looking," she said.

Her mother didn't understand. Nora Jean had to have this coat. "Please can we get it?" asked Nora Jean. "Can I use some of my Christmas money from Grandmother Rudd?" Nora Jean crossed her fingers behind her back.

Mrs. Sampson looked at her daughter and bit her lip. She sighed. "So we didn't buy you a college textbook this time. Do you want them to put your new coat in a sack or do you want to wear it?"

Outside in the parking lot, Nora Jean turned ballerina circles while her mother unlocked the car doors. "This coat was made for a life of exciting mysteries," she said.

"Is that right?" asked her mother.

Already Nora Jean was thinking. She imagined herself leaning against the school's front doors. Her eyes were cold and piercing. Her mouth was shut so tightly her lips disappeared. Jimmy Lee walked up the sidewalk. Detective Nora Jean Sampson spoke in her low, husky voice, "Beware, Jimmy Lee. I've got my eye on you." Jimmy Lee gasped. He shook from fear.

In the front seat of the car, Nora Jean turned up the collar of her new red coat. She gave her mother a great big grin. Things were looking up, she thought.

7

The Winter
Read-a-thon

At recess, Nora Jean, Rosalie, and Thomasina huddled together against the winter wind. This was the first time Nora Jean had seen her friends since the school Christmas party. She was feeling happy.

"Gee, I missed y'all," said Nora Jean. "You're my best friends in the whole world."

"I missed you, too," said Rosalie.

"I had wine in Oklahoma," said Thomasina.

This was too much for Nora Jean.

"No, you didn't," she said.

"I did, too," said Thomasina. "My grandmother cooked a chicken in cooking wine."

"Did your parents eat it?" Nora Jean knew that Thomasina's parents, just like her own parents, did not drink alcohol. They also didn't curse, although Mr. Sampson did yell "dern" and "shoot" a lot when Nora Jean watched him at his workbench in the garage. The way her father yelled them, Nora Jean thought they probably should be curse words.

"Of course, silly," said Thomasina. "Don't you know anything at all about cooking wine? All the alcohol cooks out and leaves only the flavor."

"Oh," said Nora Jean.

"But I do think that some of the alcohol was left in my chicken," Thomasina said. "Because I had a hard time walking when I got up from the table."

"Wow," said Nora Jean. Thomasina was certainly the most extraordinary friend she had. Imagine getting drunk on chicken. Nora Jean tried to think of something to impress her friend.

"Notice anything special about my new red coat?" she asked.

Thomasina glanced at her friend. "It's awful bright," she said. With that, Thomasina spotted some of the other girls. She left Nora Jean and Rosalie without even saying good-bye.

"I really like your coat," said Rosalie.

"Hum? Oh, thanks," said Nora Jean. She sighed. Thomasina had made her feel unimportant. She turned to Rosalie and pulled up her coat collar. "Do I remind you of anyone particular?"

Rosalie hesitated. "Well," she said.

"Gee whiz, don't you know anything?" asked Nora Jean, trying to sound like Thomasina. "This is a detective coat. I look like Nancy Drew," said Nora Jean.

"You sure do, Nora Jean. You look just like her," said Rosalie.

Nora Jean tightened her belt and smiled. "Thanks," she said. "Hey, here comes Jimmy Lee. I'm going to try something."

Jimmy Lee was carrying the basketball toward the blacktop. Chip, Rex, and some of the other boys were following him. Nora Jean looked around. There wasn't a door to lean on or even a wall. So she ran to the basketball hoop and leaned against the pole. In the cold air, she blew out her breath so that it would look like she was smoking.

Nora Jean tried to raise one eyebrow and glare at Jimmy Lee. "Beware, Jimmy Lee." Her low husky detective voice was squeaking. "I've got my eye on you."

"Beat it, Sampson. We want to play ball," said Jimmy Lee. He threw the ball at the hoop and barely missed Nora Jean's head.

Nora Jean stood in front of the hoop and crossed

her arms. "You don't scare me. Your days are numbered." She blew out her breath from the side of her mouth.

"You're talking crazy," he said. "Get out of the way."

Jimmy Lee dribbled the ball and stepped on her foot.

Nora Jean's idea was not going according to plan. But she still tried to appear calm, cool, and collected. She pulled up her coat collar and put one hand in her pocket. Then Nora Jean walked away from the boys.

Before she knew it, the ball bounced off her behind. She whirled around and Jimmy Lee was grinning. "Great coat, Sampson," he said, blowing on his hands. "Bull's-eye."

Rosalie met her at the edge of the blacktop and together they walked to the door. "You sure showed Jimmy Lee," said Rosalie.

Nora Jean looked sharply at her friend. "No, I didn't. You're just trying to make me feel better. I had such great hopes for this coat. I thought it made me look like a famous detective and my life would be exciting. So far, I've been ignored by Thomasina and my rear's been a moving target for a bouncing ball."

"Maybe detectives' lives are more exciting in books than in real life," said Rosalie.

Nora Jean thought a minute. "Hey, that's it," said Nora Jean. "I know what I'll do. I'll write a mystery book. Thanks a lot, Rosalie."

"Sure," Rosalie replied. "You'll write a great book."

After lunch, Mrs. Carter started a new book, *Friendly Bees, Ferocious Bees.* "One of my dearest friends wrote this book. I hope you'll enjoy it as much as I did. Maybe she can visit us sometime before the year is over," she said.

Nora Jean turned around in her seat and gave Rosalie a look. Rosalie smiled. Nora Jean sang inside her head, "Hallelujah Hiawatha! A real live author!"

After Mrs. Carter finished the first chapter, she gave a handout to the students. "Read this silently and then we'll talk about it," she said.

The paper was entitled Winter Read-a-thon. On the left side, there was a calendar for the months of January, February, and March. On the right side, Mrs. Carter had typed a letter. It said:

Dear Students,

Want to make this the best winter ever? Then join in the fun. Here's all you need to do. For the next three months, read for thirty minutes

every day, and earn yourself a party. That's right!

You can read books of your own interests, Newbery books, Texas Bluebonnet books, comic books, or the newspaper. It even counts if your parents read to you. After you have read each day, mark it off on the calendar. When you're finished, have your parents sign below and return it to school.

So, join in the fun and get ready to party, party, party. Reading is so much fun!

Sincerely,
Mrs. Carter

Nora Jean felt a sort of electricity throughout the room. All of the kids were excited. Mrs. Carter sure could make hard work seem fun.

"You're gonna give us a party?" asked Rex. He pushed up his glasses to get a better look at Mrs. Carter.

"Yes, sir," she replied.

"All right!" he said. "Hey, what's a Bluebonnet book?"

"Rex, you remember. If you read five from the state reading list, you can vote for your favorite in January," said Mrs. Carter.

"Oh, yeah, I forgot," said Rex.

"Next year's list has been announced. You may read this year's books or next year's books. It doesn't matter to me," continued Mrs. Carter,

"But I can't read for thirty minutes every day," said Chip. "I've got basketball practice and trumpet lessons."

"Here's what we'll do. I will give you a twenty minute free time. You can either catch up on your homework or you can read. Then at home, you're responsible for ten more minutes of reading. I've spoken to Mrs. King in the library and she will help you find some good books."

"Can we count what you read to us?" asked Chip.

"It counts if your parents read to you, but what I read to you does not count."

"What kind of party are we having?" asked Thomasina.

"A pizza party. Mr. Miller, Mrs. King, and I will serve you by candlelight in the elegant library café," she said smiling.

"Do you have to do it?" asked Rex.

"No," said Mrs. Carter, "you do not have to do it. It will be cheaper for me if you don't. But let me say this. If I have to buy a hundred pizzas for you readers, I'll do it gladly."

"Mrs. Carter," said Nora Jean. "I'm writing a book. Can I use part of my reading time for writing?"

From the back of the room, Nora Jean heard Jimmy Lee laugh. "Get real, Sampson," he said.

"Interesting question," said Mrs. Carter. "Let me think on it awhile and see if we can work something out. Fair enough?"

Nora Jean smiled and nodded her head.

Will Klein raised his hand.

"Yes, Will?" said Mrs. Carter.

"After our pizza party, there will be nine more weeks until summer vacation," he said.

Mrs. Carter laughed out loud. "As usual, you are correct, Mr. Klein. What on earth would I do without you?"

Nora Jean's mind was racing. There were so many things to think about—pizza parties, mysteries, red coats, reading, writing. For a terrible and boring place, sometimes school was fun.

8
Spastic Jellyfish

On an afternoon in February, Nora Jean and Rosalie stopped by the bike racks on their way home from school.

Rex was bending over his bike with his rear in the air while he fiddled with his bike chain. "Hey, Will," he called out with his head between his legs, "you doing old lady Carter's reading deal?"

"Sure I am, I'll do anything for food," Will replied.

"I wish we could do it," said a girl in Mrs. Clugg's class. "Y'all are lucky."

"Hey, Nora Jean," Chip said. "Are you and Rosalie doing it?"

"Yep," said Nora Jean.

"Me, too," said Chip.

"I thought you didn't have time," said Nora Jean.

"Well, I talked it over with my uncle," said Chip, "and he said I'd better enjoy the fun stuff while I could. He said in high school all they do is give you lots of homework and expect you to learn."

"Gee whiz," said Nora Jean.

"I'm hoping I can skip high school and go straight into college," said Chip.

"Carter said we could read anything," said Rex. "So I'm gonna read my old man's *Playboy*s."

Nora Jean's jaw dropped open in surprise. Some of the girls covered their mouths. Thomasina put her hands on her hips and glared at Rex's upside-down head. "Sinner, sinner, sinner," she said.

Jimmy Lee laughed. He was fiddling with the lock on his bike. "Way to go," he said.

"You're just gonna look at the pictures," Nora Jean said.

"Naw, I'm not. I'm going to read it," said Rex. "My dad's always telling my mom that *Playboy* has some real educational articles."

"You know that's not what Mrs. Carter meant," said Nora Jean. "You ought to be ashamed of yourself."

"Don't pay any attention to Sampson," said Jimmy Lee as he got on his bike. "She's just jealous she's not the February centerfold. But she's too skinny. Her whole body would fit in the crack of the magazine."

The girls gasped. The boys started holding their sides and laughing. A few of them even fell down on the cold winter ground. Nora Jean forgot about her promise not to look at, speak to, or forgive Jimmy Lee. She was fighting mad.

"I'll have you know, Jimmy Lee Drover, that if I wanted to I could be a model. But it just so happens I don't. I'm developing my mind. When I grow up, I'm going to be a famous author and have my picture in the encyclopedia. And one of my stories will have a slimy, dirty worm in it and I'll name it Jimmy Lee. So there." Nora Jean swished her ponytail and stuck her nose in the air.

Jimmy Lee grinned. "See you, Sampson," he said, as he took off on his bike.

Nora Jean was so mad, she went home, sat down at her desk, and wrote for an entire fifteen minutes.

The Dog Robber

Nancy Drew and her friend were walking

down the street. They saw a slimy, dirty worm crawling from a yard. He had a dog.

"That's a dog robber," Nancy Drew shouted.

"Yes," her friend said.

"Let's go get him," Nancy Drew said.

"Okay," her friend said.

Nancy Drew and her friend caught the dog robber and tied him up. That slimy, dirty worm was the dreaded Jimmy Lee.

The policeman thanked Nancy Drew and her friend. "Thanks," the policeman said.

"Anytime," Nancy Drew said. She looked down at the dog robber. "Better watch it, worm. Next time, I'm gonna step on you."

Nora Jean chewed her pencil. No doubt about it, she said to herself. I'm a genius.

But Nora Jean hadn't realized that writing was such hard work. For one thing, she had to think up all those ideas. Besides, writing made her finger bump hurt.

Mrs. Carter had told Nora Jean that she could mark off one day on the reading calendar for every five pages that she wrote. Even though her story was ab-solutely wonderful, right then and there, Nora Jean made a decision.

She was just going to have to postpone her writing

career. After all, she had to go to school. She had to do her homework. And of course she had to play. I'll try it again when I grow up and I'm not so busy, she decided.

The days and weeks slowly passed. Late in February, a snowstorm covered Fort Worth with a light blanket of snow. Schools closed for two days. Nora Jean played outside in her red coat.

On the second afternoon, she walked over to Thomasina's house.

"Now look, Nora Jean," Thomasina said. "This is how you make snow angels. I learned it in Oklahoma. Fall flat on your back. Move your arms up and down in the snow. Get real still and then jump out. There shouldn't be any footprints around your angel."

Nora Jean tried. She wanted to do it like they did in Oklahoma. Thomasina collapsed in a fit of giggles.

"What's the matter?" asked Nora Jean as she furiously waved her arms back and forth in the snow.

"Yours don't look like angels," gasped Thomasina. "They—they look like spastic jellyfish!"

Nora Jean tried to jump out of her angel that looked like a jellyfish. She tripped on her corrective shoes.

"Nora Jean, you're just so funny," giggled Thomasina.

"Why do you say that?" Nora Jean laughed, but on the inside, she wasn't feeling the least bit funny.

"Oh, you know," replied Thomasina. "Saying you're gonna be an author. And how you're always tripping on your feet. But the funniest thing is to see you and Rosalie together." Thomasina hiccupped. "We call you the toothpick and the snowball."

Nora Jean watched the sunlight sparkle in Thomasina's red hair. Her two-colored eyes looked like jewels. She was very beautiful. But all of a sudden, Nora Jean didn't want to be like Thomasina anymore.

Nora Jean brushed the snow off her red coat. She wiped her hands together. "Listen, Thomasina," she said. "You can laugh at me all you want. But if I ever hear you make fun of Rosalie again, I'll punch you in the eyes."

Thomasina kept on giggling. "See what I mean, Nora Jean. You're just so funny."

Nora Jean left. Her feelings were all mixed-up. Could a person not like her best friend, she wondered?

The weather warmed up. On a clear day in March, as Nora Jean and Rosalie walked home from school, they kicked a rock back and forth.

"You know, for two weeks Jimmy Lee hasn't teased

anybody. He doesn't even glare at people. He just sits there and reads," said Nora Jean.

"I know," said Rosalie. She crossed the street to the rock. Today, Nora Jean was slamming the rock across the street every time it was her turn. Rosalie was working up a sweat.

"I saw the 'Oprah' show the other day. This doctor said that sometimes people get very quiet right before they have a nervous breakdown," said Nora Jean. "You think Jimmy Lee is having a nervous breakdown?" She slammed the rock across the street again.

"No." Rosalie panted from across the road. "Maybe he just likes to read."

"Don't you hate Jimmy Lee?" asked Nora Jean. "He makes fun of you a lot."

"No," Rosalie said quietly. She kicked the rock in a perfect position for her friend. "I don't hate him."

"Doesn't it make you feel bad when he says tacky things to you?" This was as close as Nora Jean would get to the fact that her friend was fat. Rosalie was the one person who had never mentioned Nora Jean's skinny body. In return for this kindness, Nora Jean had never mentioned the shape of Rosalie.

"Sometimes I get my feelings hurt, but I figure he doesn't really mean it," she said.

"Well, Jimmy Lee still makes me mad, even if he is having a nervous breakdown. After all, he stole my soap dog," said Nora Jean.

Nora Jean and Rosalie stopped talking and just enjoyed kicking until they came to Rosalie's street.

Nora Jean paused. Under her breath, she asked, "What do you think about Thomasina?"

Rosalie bit her lip. She wiped the sweat from her forehead and unbuttoned her sweater. "She's very pretty and I know you like her," she said at last. Then she smiled. "See you around."

The next day in the bathroom, Nora Jean told the girls that Jimmy Lee might be having a nervous breakdown. Instead of hating him, the girls felt sorry for him.

The worst was Thomasina. She batted her eyelashes and smiled her dimpled smile and said things like, "Oh, Jimmy Lee, here's an extra cookie my Mama baked for you. You'll need it to keep up your strength."

Even though Jimmy Lee would look at Thomasina sort of strangely, he always ate the cookie and kept on reading. Maybe Nora Jean was wrong about Jimmy Lee. Maybe he really did like to read.

But now Nora Jean started worrying about her friend. She wondered if Thomasina had been getting drunk on chickens.

9
Murder
in the Library

Nora Jean wiggled her toes. For the umpteenth time, she glanced at the bulletin board above the chalkboard. Her reading calendar was still there.

She looked at the clock. The time was 1:53. Seven more minutes and they were on their way to the pizza party.

Mrs. Carter had displayed all of the finished reading calendars. A couple of them were still in good condition. Thomasina's calendar looked terrific. She had crossed out each day with a different colored Day-

Glo marker. Most of the other calendars, however, looked pitiful. There was a wide assortment of creases, wrinkles, torn corners, and ink splotches. Chip Smith's calendar looked terrible. He had left it in his jeans' pocket and his mother washed it. "It looked a lot worse. But I ironed it with spray starch," he explained.

Nora Jean's calendar was medium wrinkled and medium splotched. But Mrs. Carter said it didn't matter what the calendars looked like, so long as they were completed and signed by their parents.

At 1:55, Mrs. Elrod came in. Mrs. Elrod was a third grade teacher. She had a loud voice and laughed a lot. Whenever she was on a diet, she would ask the kids, "Y'all are going to love me when I get skinny, aren't you?" Last year, Rex had said, "We'll even love you if you get fatter." Mrs. Elrod laughed for a long time.

"Mrs. Carter, how many of your children earned the pizza party?" she asked.

"Seventeen," said Mrs. Carter, straightening some papers on her desk and pushing in her chair.

"Well, I'll be," said Mrs. Elrod. She turned to the class. "If you're going to the party, raise your hand." Seventeen hands shot up in the air.

"Good for you, Chip," she said. "I knew old Rosalie and Nora Jean could do it. Why, lookie, here. Jimmy

Lee read thirty minutes a day. I'm so happy to see such good readers. Y'all eat a piece of pizza for me, you hear? But don't make me fat, now," she laughed.

Kids smiled and nodded at Mrs. Elrod.

"Mrs. E., I have five students who will remain with you," said Mrs. Carter.

"You mean to tell me there are some turkey buzzards in this group? I want to know who didn't read every day."

Nora Jean glanced around the room. Rex was slouched down in his seat. He had his head down and his hand raised.

"Rex, is that you burying your head?" she demanded.

"Yes, ma'am," he mumbled.

"I'd be ashamed of myself, too, if I couldn't read a measly thirty minutes every day," she said. "Mrs. Carter, you just leave these children with me. In a few minutes, they're going to feel mighty sorry they didn't do their reading. Come on, you pack of buzzards."

With heads down, the five buzzards followed Mrs. E.

"Before we go," Mrs. Carter said, "I want to tell you how proud I am of your hard work. You read every single day for the past three months. It wasn't easy. You had to go to school. You had homework, ball practice, music lessons, and chores. You had to give up some of your television watching. You could have quit, but instead you persevered. You showed tenacity. You have learned two things which you will carry with you for the rest of your life. One, you have learned to love reading. And, two, you've learned that you can reach a difficult goal." Mrs. Carter's eyes watered as she blew her nose.

Nora Jean squirmed in her chair. She heard other squeaking desks. This was not the time for a long speech. Nora Jean had to help her teacher. She raised her hand.

"Yes, Nora Jean?" asked Mrs. Carter.

Nora Jean smoothed her bangs and stood up. "What we need is a song." She cleared her throat and sort of shook herself loose. "We're going to the party today, yeah! We're going to the party today, yeah!" On the word "yeah," Nora Jean wiggled her fingers and bumped her hip. The kids picked up the chant. Soon, there was a chorus of "yeahs" and finger wiggling.

Mrs. Carter wiped her eyes and laughed. "Everybody, line up," she said.

"We're going to the party today, yeah!" With quiet voices, the students chanted, wiggled, and bumped

68

their way down the hall. Mrs. Carter shushed them only once.

"Wow!" said Nora Jean when she saw the library. The lights were turned off and candles flickered from the tables. At each setting, there was a red paper place mat and a name card. Mr. Miller stood at the door with a red-checkered dish towel over his arm. He looked like a real pizza waiter.

"Welcome, ladies and gentlemen, to the library café. Find your seat and let the foods begin," he said.

The library looked great in the dark. Nora Jean couldn't see the dust. Delicious smells came from the boxes on Mrs. King's desk. Jimmy Lee was assigned to Nora Jean's table. Other than that, the party was terrific.

"Wow!" said Chip. "Am I glad my uncle talked me into this. Reading sure is fun."

Jimmy Lee nodded. He watched the grown-ups bustling around the library. "It's not bad," he agreed.

"Say, Nora Jean," said Chip. "Sing that song you just made up."

Nora Jean was pleased. She smiled her best smile at Chip. "Okay," she said. She sat up straight and opened her mouth.

"Give us a break, Sampson," said Jimmy Lee. "You look like spastic spaghetti."

Chip laughed.

Nora Jean felt her face flush. Chip had never laughed at her before. Jimmy Lee was a bad influence.

"Listen here, you little . . ." she began, but something in Jimmy Lee's eyes warned her to stop. Nora Jean turned. Mr. Miller was standing beside her.

Mr. Miller coughed and straightened the towel over his arm. "Okay, now what can I get for this fine bunch of Nolen 'Gators. Little lady, what'll it be?"

Nora Jean gulped. "Uh, pepperoni, please."

"Pepperoni on the way. Be back in a jiffy," said Mr. Miller.

Mr. Miller and Mrs. Carter passed out pizza. Mrs. King poured the soda pop. Nora Jean settled down to chewing and slurping. She noticed that kids were standing in the hall and pressing their faces against the library windows. They looked hungry. Nora Jean waved, wiped her mouth and kept on chewing.

After everybody had finished the first piece, Mr. Miller changed his way of delivering pizza.

"Okay, I've got a hamburger pizza, delicious and thick with cheese. How many for hamburger? I see five hands, five hands. Who'll make it six? I see six," called out Mr. Miller.

Kids started cramming pizza into their mouths and raising their hands for more.

"I bet I can eat ten slices," said Chip, in between bites.

"I can eat fifty slices," said Jimmy Lee.

Nora Jean was not about to be beat by Jimmy Lee. "I can eat a hundred pizzas," she declared. She crammed the crusts of her fifth slice in her mouth and swung her hand up for more.

On the sixth slice, Nora Jean lowered her head to the table and started stuffing the pizza in. She was half-finished, when she choked.

Nora Jean motioned to Chip but he was too busy chewing his own pizza. The grown-ups were busy and didn't notice. Nora Jean was beginning to panic. She couldn't breathe. Tears were streaming from her eyes.

"Can you breathe?" Jimmy Lee asked. He was looking at her strangely.

Nora Jean shook her head.

Jimmy Lee got up and stood behind Nora Jean. Then he wrapped his arms under her ribs and squeezed.

This is it, thought Nora Jean. I'm going to be murdered in the library and no one's going to notice because they're too busy stuffing their faces with pizza.

Nothing happened. Jimmy Lee squeezed harder.

So long, sweet world, Nora Jean thought. Bless Mama, Papa, and the dog I never had.

On the third try, Jimmy Lee squeezed so hard that Nora Jean thought her ribs would break. A pepperoni popped from Nora Jean's mouth.

"Finished!" yelled Mr. Miller. "The pizza's all gone. Everyone out to recess!"

Nora Jean stood up. Her knees were shaking.

"You okay?" asked Jimmy Lee.

Nora Jean nodded.

"Wow!" said Chip. "You just saved Nora Jean's life!" Chip ran for their teacher. "Hey, Mrs. Carter, Jimmy Lee just saved Nora Jean's life!"

"I thought you were trying to kill me," said Nora Jean, wiping the tears from her eyes.

Jimmy Lee laughed. "It's called the Heimlich maneuver. I read about it in the newspaper. You use it when someone is choking."

"Oh," said Nora Jean.

Chip was standing at the door of the library. "Hey, come on, Jimmy Lee. The guys are already outside," he called.

"Coming," said Jimmy Lee. "Besides, why would I want to kill you? If it wasn't for you, school would be boring." Jimmy Lee grinned and raced outside.

"Dear, are you all right?" asked Mrs. Carter. She put her hand on Nora Jean's forehead.

Nora Jean had been choked, bruised, and battered. She had tears on her face, and a burped-up pepperoni in her hand. What's more, a boy she couldn't stand had just saved her life, and in so many words told her he liked her. How on earth was she supposed to answer her teacher's question?

"I feel great," she said. Then Nora Jean burped.

10
A Real Live Author

"Hey, hero!" called Chip. "Wait up!" Chip poked Jimmy Lee on the arm. Two first grade girls ducked under Chip's arm and skipped in front of the boys. The little girls were giggling.

"May we have your autograph, Hero Jimmy Lee?" said the taller one. The shorter one kept winking at Jimmy Lee. To wink her eye, she had to wrinkle up her whole face. The little girls held hands and giggled some more.

"Not now, fans," said Chip. "The hero is busy."

Chip and Jimmy Lee pushed open the door of the library.

At the water fountain, Nora Jean watched from the corner of her eye. In less than twenty-four hours, the entire school knew that Jimmy Lee had saved Nora Jean's life. Nora Jean was glad that Jimmy Lee had helped her. But she didn't understand why everyone was making such a fuss over the soap dog thief. After all, it was only a pepperoni.

In language arts, Mrs. Carter even used the episode in their lesson on sequencing. She had Jimmy Lee stand in front of the class and discuss the steps of the Heimlich maneuver. Together, they identified the first, second, third, and fourth steps. Then Mrs. Carter made the class write a paragraph on yesterday's party, telling the events in the correct sequence. Below their paragraph, they had to draw one cartoon for each event. It was disgusting. Every single student—with the exception of Nora Jean—had a cartoon picture captioned "Nora Jean choked."

"Class," Mrs. Carter said one morning in the middle of May. "I have one final treat for you before the year is over. If you remember, I told you that one of my friends wrote the book *Friendly Bees, Ferocious Bees.* And I told you that I would see if she could visit. I'm very pleased to inform you that Anne Knox will be here a week from Wednesday. We have a lot to do before she comes. We have signs to make, books to read, and cakes to bake." Mrs. Carter smiled. "Now, what do you say we get busy?"

Nora Jean sang inside her head. "Hallelujah Hiawatha! A real live author!"

Everyday at recess, Nora Jean and the other girls worked on the signs. One was as long as the room and said NOLEN 'GATORS SAY HOWDY TO ANNE KNOX. One sign said WE LOVE BOOKS in the middle with everybody's autograph around the edges. Another sign said WELCOME TO A QUEEN BEE.

Thomasina's grandmother was going to make the cake. She was visiting from Oklahoma and knew all about cakes because she had taken a cake decorating course. Thomasina said the cake would look just like a bee.

"Is your grandmother going to put any liquor in the cake?" asked Nora Jean during recess. She was kneeling on the floor coloring a big queen bee.

"Don't be silly," said Thomasina. She was on the floor across from Nora Jean.

"Just checking," said Nora Jean.

"Although she does use vanilla extract and that has alcohol in it." Thomasina raised her eyebrows and smiled.

Nora Jean was shocked. She looked up. "It does? Will we get drunk when we eat it?"

The girls put their heads down on the floor and laughed. Nora Jean laughed, too, pretending she was making a joke. She didn't want them to know that she had been serious.

In science class, they discussed bees. Since Mrs. Carter had read the bee book aloud earlier in the year, Nora Jean remembered almost everything. She thought the body parts were interesting. Nora Jean wished that she could have a spoon-shaped tongue or some baskets on her legs. She tried to make her jaws chew sideways like a bee.

"Now, students, Anne Knox has written another book that you're going to love." Mrs. Carter's eyes were twinkling.

"What's it about?" asked Rex.

"Oh, about some wonderful little insects called cockroaches!" said Mrs. Carter.

"Eew, gross!" said Rex.

From around the room, Nora Jean heard yuks and double-yuks. Thomasina was wrinkling her nose and shaking her head.

Mrs. Carter laughed. "Did you know that cockroaches are older than dinosaurs? And did you know that sailors have always had trouble with cockroaches on ships? During the Middle Ages, ships had thousands of them. At night, the cockroaches flew around the cabins. They nibbled on the sailors' fingernails, toenails, and eyelashes."

"I'm gonna be sick!" cried Chip. Kids were holding their stomachs and groaning. But they listened to every word their teacher said.

"Tomorrow will be especially exciting. We will have a cockroach fight. Yes, it's true! Thrills and adventures await you. I've caught two cockroaches and I've made a cockroach arena. How do cockroaches fight, you ask? Well, come to school and find out." Mrs. Carter's brown eyes were dancing. "Now, boys and girls. Look me in the eye and tell me the truth. Don't you just love school?"

The class laughed. Nora Jean smiled at her teacher. "Yep," she said softly. "I guess I do."

At nine o'clock on Wednesday morning, Nora Jean and Chip were standing at the front door of R. B. Nolen Elementary looking out the windows. They were waiting for Miss Knox. Nora Jean was nervous. Chip looked nervous, too. He kept kicking at the wall.

"I sure am glad Mrs. Carter picked us to be the hosts for the author," said Nora Jean.

"Me, too," said Chip. He pulled on his collar and bow tie as he twisted his neck. "My uncle says this is a once in a lifetime opportunity."

Nora Jean looked at the signs for Anne Knox that were displayed in the hall. "Our signs look terrific, don't they?" she said.

"Yeah," said Chip.

"I wonder if she'll be driving a limousine?" asked Nora Jean.

"Probably," said Chip. "Authors are rich."

"You think she'll wear a mink coat?" asked Nora Jean.

"Naw, it's too hot."

Nora Jean and Chip stared out the windows. In a few minutes, an old beige station wagon pulled into the school driveway.

"You think that's her?" asked Nora Jean.

"Naw," said Chip. "Look at the car."

"But she's got long brown hair and that's how Mrs. Carter described her. Chip, you better run out there and be sure. If it is her, wave at me, and I'll get things ready."

"Okay," said Chip.

Chip ran out to the car, shook the lady's hand, and waved at Nora Jean. Nora Jean propped open the door and unrolled the red carpet. Actually, it wasn't carpet, it was construction paper. The school didn't have any red carpet, so Nora Jean had taped sheets of red construction paper together. Quickly she examined it. If Nora Jean squeezed her eyelids shut, then barely opened them and crossed her eyes, the red construction paper looked exactly like red carpet.

"Miss Knox," said Chip, fiddling with his bow tie. "May I present Nora Jean Sampson."

"How do you do," said Nora Jean. She curtsied. "Did you leave your limousine at home?"

Miss Knox laughed. "I'm afraid I don't have one."

"Oh," said Nora Jean. She was disappointed. Miss Knox's car looked so ordinary. She stared at Miss Knox to see if she looked like an author. "Welp, I can tell you're not a teacher."

"How is that?" asked Miss Knox.

"Because you're wearing high heels," she said.

Inside, Nora Jean and Chip introduced Miss Knox to the secretary, Mr. Miller, the nurse, and the sick kid on the nurse's bed. Then, Nora Jean and Chip took her by the arms and steered her to the hall.

"Here are the signs we made for you," said Chip. "Nora Jean helped design them."

"These are wonderful," said the author.

Nora Jean smiled and tried not to look too big for her britches.

"Nora Jean is real talented. She's also a song writer," said Chip.

"Oh, really? I'd love to hear one."

"Well, as a matter of fact, I made up one for you. It goes like this. 'Hallelujah Hiawatha! It's a real live author!' " As Nora Jean sang, she pranced around in a circle and beat her chest.

"Oh, my," said Anne Knox. She looked as if she was trying not to laugh. Either that or she was about to sneeze.

"You see what I mean? Nora Jean is real talented," said Chip.

Nora Jean shrugged her shoulders. "It's a gift."

Right then, Mrs. Tennison brought her class for their morning water break. To be polite, Nora Jean and Chip introduced every first grader to the famous author.

Jimmy Lee hurried up to them. "Is that her?" he whispered.

"Yeah," said Chip. "She doesn't have a limousine but she seems okay."

"Well, put a move on it. Mrs. Carter sent me to find you," said Jimmy Lee.

Nora Jean and Chip took Miss Knox by the arms and led her to the room. Will Klein was waiting at the front of the class.

"On behalf of our class," said Will Klein, "we would like to present you with an R. B. Nolen 'Gator T-shirt and this certificate making you an honorary Alligator. And after you speak, we hope you will partake of some delicious bee cake." The class clapped and Will sat down.

Miss Knox glanced at the table covered in yellow paper, at the white, black, and yellow bee cake, and at the bee poems stapled above the chalkboard. Then she looked at the students.

"I have never had a more wonderful welcome," she said. "My hosts greeted me at the door with a red carpet. Your signs are wonderful. The cake looks delicious. And these bee poems are unique. Thank you very, very much."

The class clapped again.

For the next forty-five minutes, Anne Knox talked about honeybees, cockroaches, and some of her other books. Nora Jean listened to every word. Miss Knox paused. "I've talked long enough," she said. "Do you have any questions?"

"How many books have you done wrote?" Rex asked.

"Published or unpublished?" Miss Knox smiled. "I've had five published and I've written many more that are in my filing cabinet."

"Why did you write about roaches?" someone asked.

Miss Knox's eyes twinkled. "Everybody loves roaches, don't they?" she asked.

"Eew-yuk!" groaned the class.

"Where did you get the idea for the cockroach fight?" someone else asked.

"I found the idea in a college textbook. When I tried it, both cockroaches touched each other with their antennae. Then one cockroach kicked the other one and raised himself so that he was taller than his opponent," she said.

The class nodded. They had noticed the same actions.

"Do you like to write?" asked Nora Jean. She smoothed her bangs. "I was going to be a writer, but I was too busy."

From the back of the room, Nora Jean heard Jimmy Lee snicker.

"Interesting question," said Miss Knox. "I write because I like to think. But thinking is so hard that sometimes I goof off. I have to make time to write. If I don't, I'm like you, Nora Jean. I tell myself that I'm too busy."

Nora Jean felt proud. She and a real live author had something in common. Nora Jean turned around and gave Rosalie a happy look. She ignored Jimmy Lee.

"Do you get mugged at airports?" asked Chip.

"Pardon me?" said Miss Knox. "I'm not sure I understand."

"You know. Since you're so famous. Do people mug you and ask for your autograph?"

Miss Knox burst out laughing. "Oh, Chip. I hope I haven't disappointed you. But I'm really not famous at all. I'm just an ordinary person."

Nora Jean sprang to Miss Knox's defense. It was true that Miss Knox didn't have a fancy car and she probably didn't own a mink coat. Still, she was special. "Well, at least you're a live author instead of a dead one," said Nora Jean.

Everybody laughed. After a few minutes, Mrs. Carter wiped her eyes. "Why don't we all have some cake?"

"All right!" said a few of the boys in the back row.

Will Klein raised his hand. "Mrs. Carter, may I remind you that this is a double celebration. If you don't count weekends, there's only eleven more days till summer vacation."

11

12 Whole Weeks of Summer Vacation

"BRRING-RING!" rang the bell. And with that bell, the last day of school was over. For thirty-eight weeks—or forty weeks—if you counted the winter vacation, Nora Jean had waited for this very moment. She was happy, excited, and also a little bit sad.

"Class, you are a wonderful group of students, and I love you dearly." Mrs. Carter smiled. She blew her nose. "I won't keep you with a long speech, today." She paused. Her eyes began to twinkle. "Will, do you have one final comment before we go?"

Will Klein grinned. "Give or take a few days, we've

got twelve whole weeks of summer vacation!" he yelled.

Everyone cheered. Over the shouts, Mrs. Carter said, "Class dismissed!"

"Nora Jean," called Thomasina. "Help me carry my things. You can come back for your stuff later."

Nora Jean looked at her beautiful friend. "Do it yourself, Thomasina. I'm busy."

Nora Jean raced to the bike rack. She had some unfinished business to take care of.

"Hey, Nora Jean, you gotta end-of-school song for us?" asked Chip.

"Uh, no, not today," said Nora Jean. She was looking for Jimmy Lee. He was fiddling with his bike chain.

"Uh, Jimmy Lee, there's something I've been meaning to say to you," she said in a rush. "And I'm sorry I didn't tell you earlier, but I was never going to speak to you again." Nora Jean looked down at the giant Jimmy Lee. "Thank you for saving my life. So there."

"Sure," said Jimmy Lee.

"And there's something else. I've been thinking all along that you were a soap dog stealer. I'm sorry. There's probably a good explanation."

Jimmy Lee grinned. "Nope," he said. "I took it."

Nora Jean's eyes blazed. She glared a hole through Jimmy Lee. "I knew it!" she yelled.

"Sure," he said. "Yours looked a lot better than the

one I made. Besides, I left you mine. What more could you want?" Jimmy Lee grinned again.

"You just beat everything, you know that, Jimmy Lee? Why, I oughta . . ."

"Sampson," said Jimmy Lee, interrupting her. "There's something I've been meaning to say to you."

"What's that, creephead?" she said.

"I think you're swell," said Jimmy Lee.

"Hey, Nora Jean," called Chip as he popped a wheelie with his bike, "I'm gonna miss your songs this summer."

Nora Jean looked at Chip. She looked at Jimmy Lee. "Well, I, uh, I'll . . . it's like . . ." Nora Jean sputtered. "Oh, fuzz-bucket." She swished her ponytail and headed for home.

"See you in September," called Jimmy Lee.

"Bye, Nora Jean," said Chip.

Nora Jean ran to catch up with Rosalie. "By the way," she said. "Have I mentioned that you're my very best friend?" She jumped up and clicked the heels of her corrective shoes together.

Rosalie smiled. "I already knew."

With her back to the boys, Nora Jean grinned. Her heart was soaring. She pitched her book bag in the air and caught it. Welp, Nora Jean said to herself, twelve weeks of summer vacation is going to be a very long time.